Nina Crews

I'M NOT NOT SMALL

 Greenwillow Books, *An Imprint of* HarperCollins*Publishers*

Illustrations for this book were digitally drawn and collaged
in Adobe Photoshop, incorporating photographs and textures
created by the artist.
The text type is Sofia Pro Light.

Library of Congress Cataloging-in-Publication Data is available.
ISBN 978-0-06-305826-2 (hardback)

22 23 24 25 26 RTLO 10 9 8 7 6 5 4 3 2 1
First Edition

 Greenwillow Books

To Asa

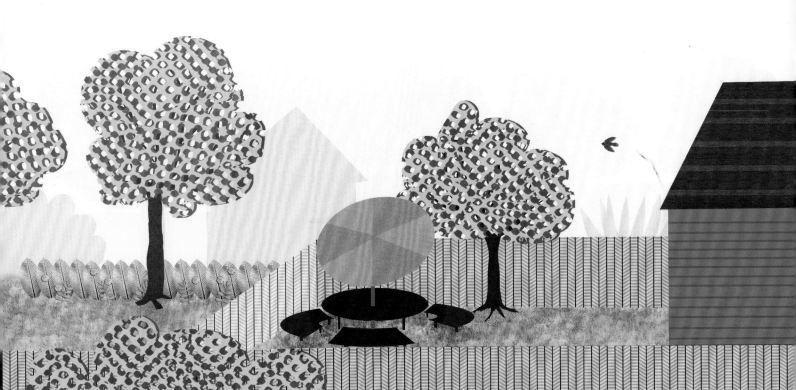

Sunshine! Daytime!
I want to play outside.

"Go ahead," says my mother.
"You're a big kid now."

I am big!
And I am going outside
on my own!

But the sky is big.
The trees are big.
The backyard is big.

I am small.

I am not small!

My dog is small.
See how tall I am
when I stand on my toes?

My cat is small.

My dog likes to lick my cat
with her big, pink tongue.

My rabbit is small.

I pet him gently,
so he does not get scared.

Sparrows are small.

They eat seeds from our bird feeder,
and their voices go *tweet, tweet,
tweet, tweet, tweet!*

That bee is small.
And scary!

I will be brave
and stay very still,
while it looks at me.

This ant is small.

It is really, really, really small.
I could crush it with my foot!

But I won't.
I will watch it carry a big crumb.

I am big!

I am bigger
than the ant,
the bee,
the sparrows,
my rabbit,
my cat,
and my dog!

I like being big.

"Hey, big guy! Are you ready for breakfast?"

I like being big.
But sometimes I am
happy to be small.